Sapa and Martha Make an Amaut

WRITTEN BY
Shavanna Oogaaq and Emily Jackson
ILLUSTRATED BY
Charlene Chua

Sapa smiled at her reflection in the window as she walked into the front office of her school. Her mouth always looked and felt so clean after she went to the dentist. She followed her *ataata** into the office so that he could sign her into school. Her appointment was during lunch, so she was late coming back to class.

Sapa heard someone else come into the office behind her. She turned around to see Martha and her ataata. She was getting signed in late, too.

Both girls headed down the hall to their classroom. Sapa was a little nervous. Martha had not seemed to like Sapa very much when Sapa first moved to town, but they were getting along better now.

***ataata** (a-TAA-ta): father

"Why are you late?" Sapa asked Martha.

"Airport. My *anaana** is flying out to have her baby," Martha replied.

"Wow!" Sapa said. "That's exciting!"

Martha smiled and raised her eyebrows in response.

As the girls entered their classroom, they saw everyone spread out, working in pairs. Their teacher explained that the school was putting on a fashion show as part of the spring festival. Each group would need to design and make an article of clothing to display in the fashion show.

"You two will be our last group!" their teacher said.

"So…what do you want to make?" asked Sapa as the girls found a place on the floor. Sapa had a million ideas running through her head. She grabbed a pencil and started drawing.

***anaana** (a-NAA-na): mother

"We could make a cape! Or a really cool coat with a bunch of secret pockets to put stuff in. Or what about *nanuq** pants? I've always wanted to have nanuq pants," Sapa said quickly, drawing her ideas as fast as she could think of them.

"I don't know," said Martha. "Maybe…I don't know." Sapa looked up from her drawing. Martha hesitated for a minute, and then she spoke.

"Can we make an *amaut*?"**

***nanuq** (na-NUQ): polar bear
****amaut** (a-MOWT): Inuinnaqtun term for a woman's parka with a pouch for carrying a child

Sapa wasn't exactly sure what an amaut was.

"Is an amaut like an *amauti*?* Or am I messing up my Inuktitut again?" she asked.

"You're right! They look a bit different, but they both carry babies," Martha said. "I want to make an amaut like my anaana has. My biological anaana, anyway. Paula. She's from Kugluktuk."

"I didn't know that you were adopted," Sapa blurted out.

Martha just shrugged. "I am. So can we make the amaut?"

Sapa didn't think it would be as exciting as a coat with secret pockets or polar bear pants. But she was happy that Martha was being friendly.

***amauti** (a-MOW-ti): woman's parka with a pouch for carrying a child

"All right! Let's do it. What does an amaut look like in Kugluktuk?" Sapa asked as she handed Martha a pencil.

"It's like this," Martha explained as she drew a picture of the amaut. It looked different than the ones Sapa saw around town. "I have an amaut from Paula. She carried me in it for a while. It's at home, but I'll bring it tomorrow," Martha said.

"Cool!" Sapa said. Martha raised her eyebrows in agreement and smiled a bit.

"You wanna come over and help me find it?" Martha asked. "Maybe we can use it to make a pattern."

"Yes!" Sapa exclaimed.

After school, the girls stopped at Martha's house to pick up her amaut. Sapa looked curiously at the pictures on Martha's wall while Martha searched for the amaut. There was a picture of Martha and her parents, and a picture of Martha and her friends. And then Sapa saw a picture of Martha smiling with a man and a woman and two older kids.

Sapa tapped the picture gently. "Is this your biological family?"

Martha came over to look at the picture. "Yep," she said. She pointed to the adults. "That's Paula and Fred." Then she pointed to the kids. "And my siblings, Aislyn and Braden."

"It must be so nice to have two families!" Sapa thought out loud. "I only have one."

Martha shrugged. "It's good," she said. "It's like I'm not even adopted most of the time. My parents are my parents, even if they didn't have me." Martha paused for a minute. "But I care about my biological parents, too. I want them to be proud of me," Martha said as she looked at the picture.

Well, of course they'll be proud! Sapa thought. *Why would they not be proud?* Before Sapa could ask more questions, Martha went to the closet and continued searching for the amaut.

"Look, here it is!" Martha exclaimed. They both admired the amaut. It looked just like Martha's drawing!

The next day at school, Martha and Sapa stared at the amaut spread out on the table in front of them.

"Do you know how to make a pattern?" Martha asked.

"Nope. Do you?" Sapa replied. Martha scrunched her nose. The girls asked Alice for help. Alice was an Elder who was helping the class with their projects.

Alice came over to their table and looked at the amaut from all angles, inside and out. As the girls watched closely, she carefully drew some large shapes onto big sheets of paper. Then she handed them to Sapa and Martha to cut out.

They laid their paper patterns over the green fabric they had chosen and cut out the shapes. Martha started sewing the body of the amaut. Since it looked like Martha needed to focus, Sapa moved to a table with some other kids and began working on the belt.

This is fun, Sapa thought. *I can talk and sew at the same time!*

Sapa was busy telling a story to the other kids when she heard Martha sigh and grumble. *Uh oh,* Sapa thought. *I'd better go see what's wrong.*

"I can't do it," Martha said, throwing her sewing down onto the table. "It's too hard. I'll never be able to make an amaut good enough for the fashion show." Martha's eyes started to fill with tears.

Sapa looked at the amaut. The stitches were a little bit crooked and the fabric bunched a little, but Sapa thought it was looking pretty great. Sapa wondered if something more than the sewing was bothering Martha.

Sapa crouched down by Martha's chair. "I think it looks pretty good," Sapa said. "Is there something else wrong?"

Martha scrunched her nose. "I don't want to talk about it," she said.

"Okay," Sapa replied. "If you're sure. But when I'm upset, talking about what's bothering me usually helps me feel better."

Martha didn't say anything for a minute, but Sapa stayed with her. Eventually, Martha started to speak. "I just want to make a good amaut to show Paula," Martha said quietly. "I want her to be proud of me."

Sapa thought for a moment. "Why do you think she wouldn't be proud of you?" Sapa asked.

"I don't know," said Martha. She paused, and then said, "I know all my parents love me. But sometimes I feel like my biological parents didn't want me, and that's why they didn't keep me. I thought if I could make a good amaut that looks like Paula's, maybe she would see that I'm good enough."

At first, Sapa didn't know what to say. *My parents kept me,* she thought, *so I don't know that feeling.* She thought some more. *But...I do know what it's like to feel not good enough. And I know what helps me get through that feeling.*

Sapa looked up at her friend and asked, "Would you like a hug?" Martha raised her eyebrows in agreement. Sapa gave her the best hug she could give.

"Sometimes I don't feel like I'm good enough either," Sapa said.

"But you're good at everything!" Martha protested. "Why would you feel that way?"

"Remember last year when I first moved back to Kuugaapik? I had been living in the south since I was a kid, and I didn't know very much Inuktitut. When you guys spoke Inuktitut around me and I couldn't understand, I felt like I wasn't good enough," Sapa responded. "I thought you didn't want me around."

Martha thought for a moment. "I didn't think of it that way," she said. "I'm sorry we weren't nicer to you."

"That's okay," Sapa said and smiled. "When I was feeling unwanted and like I wasn't good enough, I told my anaana. We talked for a long time. She said that all I could do was try every day to learn a little bit more, but that she loved me no matter what. As I practised, I felt better and better," Sapa said. "I know it's not exactly the same, but I think talking to someone when you're upset is a good idea. It lets the bad feelings escape."

By this time, Alice had come and sat down beside Martha. She quietly picked up the amaut and looked at Martha's stitches.

"Should we try again?" Alice asked. Martha wiped her face and raised her eyebrows.

Alice showed Martha a new stitch to try, and then handed the fabric back over. Martha began to stitch her amaut again, and Sapa sat with her and worked on the belt.

"You know, when I was younger, my brother and his wife adopted my last daughter," Alice said. Sapa and Martha looked up at her, but Alice nodded at them so they would keep working.

"They couldn't have a child of their own, and they were very sad. I knew my daughter could give them love and spread it around wherever she went," Alice said. "I missed her, but I knew she would bring happiness to more people."

"Really? So you always wanted her?" Martha asked Alice.

"Oh, yes," Alice said. "And I still want her and love her. Even if I don't see her very often, I am proud of the love she has brought to people around her."

Sapa watched a smile spread across Martha's face. Martha worked even more carefully on their amaut. Alice smiled at Sapa and walked over to help some other students.

One month later, the fashion show was about to begin. Sapa, wearing a camera around her neck, fixed the hood of the amaut on Martha's back. Martha's anaana had gently tucked Martha's brand-new baby brother into the pouch, and he was sleeping away.

"I'm so nervous to show everyone!" Martha said. "Do you think it's good enough?" Then Martha stopped and shook her head. "Actually, I know it's good enough. All of my parents will love it." Sapa grinned. She gave Martha a high five for good luck. Then she ran into the audience to watch the show.

Sapa watched all her classmates walk by with their beautiful clothing. When Martha walked by her parents, wearing her amaut with her new little brother in it, Sapa snapped a picture of her, so Martha could send it to Paula to show off their beautiful amaut. She had never seen her new friend Martha smile so big.

Inuktitut Glossary

Notes on Inuktitut pronunciation: There are some sounds in Inuktitut that may be unfamiliar to English speakers. The pronunciations below convey those sounds in the following ways:

- A double vowel (for example, *aa, ee*) creates a long vowel sound.
- Capitalized letters indicate the emphasis.
- **q** is a "uvular" sound, which is a sound that comes from the very back of the throat (the uvula). This is different from the **k** sound, which is the same as the typical English **k** sound.

For more Inuktitut and Inuinnaqtun pronunciation resources, please visit inhabiteducation.com/inuitnipingit.

amaut a-MOWT	**Inuinnaqtun term for a woman's parka with a pouch for carrying a child**
amauti a-MOW-ti	**woman's parka with a pouch for carrying a child**
anaana a-NAA-na	**mother**
ataata a-TAA-ta	**father**
nanuq na-NUQ	**polar bear**